Nate the Great
and the
Monster
Mess

Nate the Great
and the
Monster
Mess

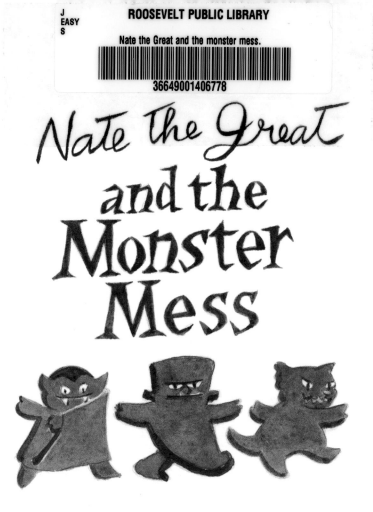

by Marjorie Weinman Sharmat

illustrated by Martha Weston

in the style of Marc Simont

A Yearling Book

Published by
Yearling
an imprint of
Random House Children's Books
a division of Random House, Inc.
New York

Visit us on the Web! www.randomhouse.com/kids

Educators and librarians, for a variety of teaching tools, visit us at
www.randomhouse.com/teachers

ISBN-13: 978-0-440-41662-3
ISBN-10: 0-440-41662-0

Reprinted by arrangement with Delacorte Press
Printed in the United States of America
One Previous Edition
September 2005
23 22 21 20

For ANNA RICHARDSON WEINMAN,
the world's best mother,
who, by the way,
created the world's best chocolate cookie
—M.W. S.

To my CBI buddies—
Mira, Dwight, Susan, and Ashley
—M.W.

Chapter One
Draculas, Frankensteins, and Werewolves!

My name is Nate the Great.

I am a detective.

My dog, Sludge, is a detective too.

Today Sludge and I had big plans.

To do nothing.

Suddenly I saw something.

There was a note under the door
of my room.

It was written in scribbles.

I knew it was from my mother.

She scribbles when she is in a hurry.

I read it.

Dear Nate the Great,
I lost my RECIPE for
MONSTER COOKIES.
It is on a LONG piece
of paper. I looked
INSIDE the house.
Now I must look OUTSIDE.
When I find the paper
I will be back.
Love,
Your Mother

"I love those monsters,"
I said to Sludge.
"Strawberry Draculas,
Chocolate Frankensteins,
Cinnamon Werewolves.
My mother hates the werewolves,
but she bakes them for me anyway.
I must find that recipe."

I, Nate the Great,
had never solved a case
for my mother.
My mother knew
where everything was.
Until now.
"We will look inside,"
I said. "Perhaps my mother
did not look everywhere in the house."

I, Nate the Great, liked this case.
I could stay home.
I would not have to see
Rosamond or her four cats.
I would not have to see
Annie's dog, Fang.
I could make as many pancakes
as I wanted.

Chapter Two
The Long and Short of It

Sludge and I went to the kitchen.
My mother kept her recipes there.
Each short recipe was written
on one side of a card.
Each long recipe was written
on one side
of a long piece of paper.

The cards were in one pile.
The papers were in another.
My mother liked the cards.
They were all neat and clean.
She did not like the papers.
They were crinkled, wrinkled,
and stained with food.
The pile of papers was a mess.
And it was huge!
But I, Nate the Great,
had to look for Monster Cookies.
"The recipe should be easy
to find," I said to Sludge.
"It's the only one with
drawings of werewolves.
Dozens and dozens of werewolves.
All crossed out.
My mother has never seen
a werewolf she likes."

I spread every sheet on the floor.
I found recipes for foods
I had never eaten
and would never want to eat.
Like Squash Slosh.
I found great names like
Chocolate Bumps and Pecan Plops.
I found scribbled names
that I had never heard of.
Like Lemfan.

There was nothing listed under that one.
And Fig Fizzle.
Nothing was listed under that either.
There were more pages
with scribbled names.
Maybe the recipes
would be added later.
I, Nate the Great,
could not find
Monster Cookies.

Chapter Three
One Big Mess

It was time to think.
I made some pancakes.
I gave Sludge a bone.
We ate and thought.
I knew that my mother
had not made Monster Cookies
for a week.
Today she'd discovered that the
recipe was gone.
So the recipe might have
been missing for a week
or less than a week.

I turned to Sludge.
"We will look in every nook
and cranny of this house.
Look hard. It's for my mother."
Sludge and I looked, sniffed,
climbed up, bent down,
knocked things over,
pulled things out,
pushed things around.

We crumbled stuff.
We jumbled stuff.
Nothing.

"I, Nate the Great, say
there is a big clue
missing in this case.
The clue is my mother.
We have to find her
and ask her questions."

Sludge and I walked toward
the front door.
"Ouch!"
We stumbled over the mess
we had made.

"We will clean this up
when we get back," I said.

Chapter Four
Tasty in Lemon

We went outside.
"Think about where
my mother would go," I said.
Sludge sat down.
"No, don't *sit* and think.
Walk and think," I said.
Suddenly I knew why
Sludge had sat down.
Fang was up ahead with Annie.
I went up to Annie.
"I am looking for my mother,"
I said. "Or her recipe
for Monster Cookies.

Have you seen either one?"
"I saw your mother
three days ago," Annie said.
"She said hello.
Then she looked at Fang.

She kept staring at him.
Then she took a
long piece of paper
out of her pocketbook
and wrote something down.
She said that Fang
would be tasty in lemon.
What did that mean?"
"You wouldn't want to know,"
I said.

Chapter Five
The Best Follow

Sludge and I walked on.
"Maybe my mother is adding
Fang to her list of
tasty monsters," I said.
"I can hardly wait to eat him.
But that does not
help us find my mother."
Sludge turned around.
"Where are you going?" I asked.
Sludge led the way to Oliver's house.
Oliver lives next door.

Oliver is a pest.

Oliver follows people.

Oliver follows animals.

Oliver follows the world.

Oliver was in his yard.

"Oliver," I said.

"Did you follow my mother today?"

"Your mother went out today?"

Oliver said. "Oh, phooey, I missed her!

Your mother is a great follow.
She goes to good places.
Like the fish store."
Oliver collects eels.
He likes anything fishy.
"Oliver," I said, "did you
follow my mother this week?"
"Yes. Three days ago.
It was my favorite follow
of the month."
"Where did she go?"
Oliver looked proud.
He opened a box.
He took out a card.

"I know who I follow
and when I follow them
and where they go," he said.
"I have a card for everybody.
Let's see.

NATE THE GREAT'S MOTHER.

Thursday. 2 P.M.

She spoke to Annie.

She looked at Fang.

She took a long piece of paper
out of her pocketbook.

She scribbled something on it.

It was probably her grocery list.

She went to
the supermarket next.

She looked at the paper.

Then she took a jar
of cinnamon from a shelf.

She stared at the jar.

She put it back.
She bought chocolate,
strawberries, and a lemon."
"A lemon?" I said.
Was she *really* going to make
Lemon Fang Cookies?
"What happened next?" I asked.
"She went to the fish store,"
Oliver said. "She took more long papers
from her pocketbook,
looked at them, and bought
lots of fish."
"Aha!" I said. "More long papers.
They could not be grocery lists.
They must have been recipes.
At the fish store for fish dishes.
At the supermarket
for Monster Cookies.
What did she do next?"

"I don't know," Oliver said.
"I had to go home
and feed my eels."
"I must go to the fish store," I said.
"I must follow you," Oliver said.
"I know it," I said.

Chapter Six
Something Fishy

Sludge and I walked
to the fish store.
Oliver followed us.
Rosamond and her four cats
were there.
Rosamond was buying tuna.
"Here," she said
to the man behind the counter,
"is some paper to wrap my tuna in.
You wrapped my fish in it
two months ago.
But the other side hasn't been used.
Just turn the paper over
and use the other side."

The paper was stained,
rumpled, and crumpled.
And smelly.
The man made a face.
But he wrapped the tuna
in the paper.
"I recycle everything,"
Rosamond said. "But fish paper
is the best."
I, Nate the Great,
was disgusted to hear that.
I went up to Rosamond.
I did not want to do that.
"Have you seen my mother?
Or her recipe for
Monster Cookies?" I asked.
Rosamond looked mad.
"I saw your mother
a few minutes ago.

She asked me if I
had seen her recipe.
Now *you* are asking me questions.
You always ask me questions.

From now on I will
charge you for my answers."
Rosamond was strange.
Now I, Nate the Great, had
to be even stranger.
"Well, from now on,
I, Nate the Great,
will charge you
for my questions," I said.
Rosamond shrugged.
"Okay, no charge," she said.
"The answer is that I have not
seen your mother's recipe.
And I don't know
where she went
after I saw her."
"For *that* you wanted money?" I said.
Rosamond hugged her tuna package.

"Well, when I answer your questions
I have to think hard,
I have to breathe harder,
my toes tingle,
my cats get hungry,
my . . ."

It was time to leave.
Sludge, Oliver, and I went outside.

Oliver took out a card
and scribbled something on it.
Hmmm.
It was just the way my mother
scribbled her short recipes
on *her* cards.

Sludge sniffed the card.
Was he thinking what I was thinking?

Chapter Seven
Crossed-Out Werewolves!

Sludge and I rushed home.

"We have solved the case," I said.

I opened the front door.

We tripped.

"We'll clean up soon,"
I said. "But first we
have to use our clues.
We know that my mother
had the recipe when she
went to the supermarket
three days ago.
She almost bought cinnamon there.
But she didn't.
My mother really *hates*
Cinnamon Werewolves.
So she must have decided
not to bake them anymore.
And that meant she didn't need
all those crossed-out werewolves!
I, Nate the Great, say that without them,
the Monster Cookies recipe
was short enough to write on a card.

So when my mother got home,
she copied the recipe
from the piece of paper
onto a card.
She threw out the paper.
Then she forgot that
the recipe is now on a card."
I went to the pile of cards.
I thumbed through them fast.
I knew I would find
Monster Cookies.
Sludge wagged his tail.
He knew it too.

I looked once.

I looked twice.

I looked three times.

Sludge stopped wagging.

"The recipe is not
on a card," I said.

"I should have known
that my mother *knows*
what she is looking for.
A long piece of paper."

I opened a cupboard.

There was plenty of cinnamon.

My werewolves were safe.

"We have to keep looking
for my mother," I said.

Chapter Eight
The Right Place

Sludge and I rushed to the door.
Thud! Bump! Thump!
We fell down.
"We will clean up
this place soon," I said.
Sludge was tired of hearing that.
We sat there.

"It's hard work being
a detective," I said.

"I have to think about
what I am looking for
and *who* I am working for.
I am working for my mother.
I know that she does not lose things.
She puts things in the right place.
The right place for that recipe
was with the other papers.
She must have put it there three days ago.
So why wasn't it *there*?"
Sludge didn't know.
Neither did I, Nate the Great.
What was important in this case?

Was it important
that my mother had scribbled
something
on a long piece of paper
after she saw Fang?
Was it important
that she bought chocolate,
strawberries, a lemon,
and lots of fish?
Fish could not have anything
to do with Monster Cookies.
Still, there was a clue
at the fish store.
I, Nate the Great,
felt it in my bones.
And up my nose.
It had something to do
with Rosamond's fish paper.

Chapter Nine
A Scribble
Among Scribbles

"Get up!" I said to Sludge.
"We have the clues we need.
Fish paper and lemon."
Sludge and I made our way
back to the kitchen.
I looked at the papers
spread over the floor.

I found the sheet that had
Lemfan scribbled on it.
The paper was stained,
wrinkled, and crinkled.

Just like Rosamond's fish paper.
Because it had already been used
on the other side!
To make cookies.
I turned the paper over.
I, Nate the Great,
read what I knew I would read . . .

Monster Cookies!
There it was.
How to make Strawberry Draculas,
Chocolate Frankensteins,
and Cinnamon Werewolves.
"This case is solved," I said.
"Here is what happened.
My mother had some recipes
with her when she saw Annie and Fang.

She scribbled a note
to buy lemon
on the back of
the Monster Cookies recipe.
Lemfan.
Short for *Lemon Fang* Cookies.
After she shopped and came home,
she put the recipes back on the pile.
But because she had scribbled
on the back of
the Monster Cookies recipe,
it was turned *down*
instead of *up*.
The next couple of days
my mother used other recipes
from the pile.
The pile became very messy.
Today my mother was ready
to make the cookies.

She went to the pile.
She was in a hurry.
She thumbed through
lots of recipes and scribbles.
Like Lemfan.
A scribble among scribbles.
My mother passed it by.
Just the way I did.
If the paper had been blank
we would have known
it was the wrong side.
I, Nate the Great, say that
in this case
nothing would have
been better
than something."
I heard the front door open.
I clutched the Monster Cookies recipe.

I had a big surprise
to show my mother.
I heard a scream.
I was glad that I did not hear
a thud or a bump or a thump.
Sludge looked scared.
I, Nate the Great,
now knew that I
had one more surprise
for my mother
than I wanted.

Sludge and I
were very busy
for the rest of the day.

~Extra~
Fun Activities!

What's Inside

NATE'S NOTES: Monsters

VAMPIRES are monsters that suck human blood. Yuck! Legends about vampires started hundreds of years ago. But back then, people believed vampires were real. In the 1730s, newspapers in Hungary reported vampire sightings.

4

After the 1700s, people forgot about vampires. Then a writer named Bram Stoker wrote a scary book for grown-ups called <u>Dracula</u>. The book was first printed in 1897. Millions of people read it. The story became a stage play. Later it was made into a movie. Vampires became part of our culture.

Now there are kids' books about vampires. There are TV shows like <u>Buffy the Vampire Slayer.</u> Sometimes vampires are even funny, like the Count on <u>Sesame Street.</u>

FRANKENSTEIN comes from a book too. A woman named Mary Shelley wrote it. It was first published in 1818. Shelley based the story on a scary dream she had one night after reading too many ghost stories.

A WEREWOLF is a person who turns into a wolf. (Were used to mean "man" in English a long time ago.) Some werewolves change at will. Others change under a full moon. Werewolf legends exist around the world. In some places, the person turns into a bear, a hyena, or another fierce creature.

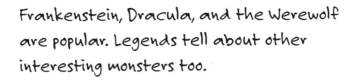

Frankenstein, Dracula, and the Werewolf are popular. Legends tell about other interesting monsters too.

BIGFOOT (or SASQUATCH) is a hairy, apelike giant that lives in the woods of California.

The YETI of the Himalayan Mountains (also known as the ABOMINABLE SNOWMAN) is another scary, hairy ape.

For more than thirteen hundred years, people have been claiming that a monster lives in Scotland's Loch Ness. NESSIE looks something like a big dinosaur, with a long neck and two humps.

Another dino look-alike is the MOKELE-MBEMBE, which has been spotted in swampy central Africa. This monster is described as big, hairy, and smelly. Well, you wouldn't expect a monster to wear perfume, would you?

Nate's Notes: Stuff About Eels

Some people—like Oliver—keep eels as pets. Other people eat them grilled on rice. Eels are fish that look like snakes. They are long and skinny and seem to slither through the water.

There are about five hundred species of eel. All start life as eggs floating freely in the ocean.

Then they develop into larvae. Eel larvae look very different from grown-up eels. Scientists used to think they were different species. Eel larvae look like leaves with eyes. Some eels stay in their larval form for two and a half years! Eel eggs and larvae always live in salt water.

Eel larvae go through an amazing change before becoming adults. It's called a metamorphosis. Their bodies get smaller and tube-shaped. Their teeth fall out. Their snouts become rounded. Other changes happen too, depending on the species.

Grown-up eels can be as small as four inches long—or as big as eleven and a half feet long!

Some adult eels live in the ocean. Other eels live in freshwater—like lakes and rivers.

Eels aren't the only creatures that undergo metamorphosis. Did you know that:

Tadpoles ──→ Frogs

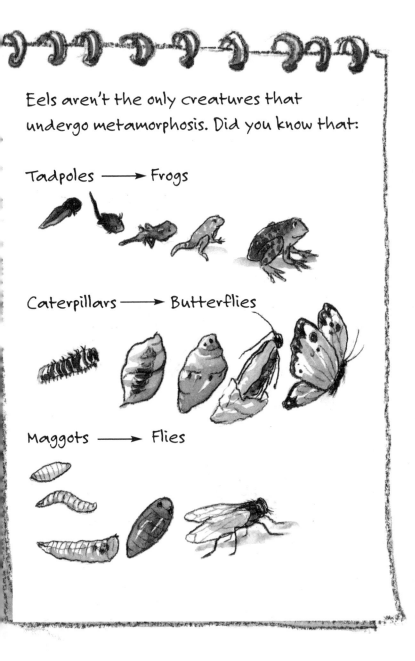

Caterpillars ──→ Butterflies

Maggots ──→ Flies

Green moray eels are actually blue eels covered with a layer of yellow slime. They have sharp teeth and like to bite. And they are poisonous!

Some eel species can travel short distances over land. Why? To catch and eat frogs and lizards.

Some eels are electric! They work like big batteries. One twenty-foot eel is powerful enough to light twelve lightbulbs. Electric eels live in the Amazon and in other rivers in South America. They can be dangerous.

How to Make
Lemon Fang Cookies

Taking a bite out of a Fang-shaped cookie is fun. (And it's much better than having Fang take a bite out of you.)

Ask an adult to help you with this recipe. It will make about three dozen Fangs.

You need an oven to bake the cookies.

GET TOGETHER:

- a mixing bowl
- an electric mixer
- aluminum foil
- a dog-shaped cookie cutter (the scarier, the better!)
- stuff to decorate your cookies (see pages 20 and 21 for ideas)
- a rolling pin
- cookie sheets

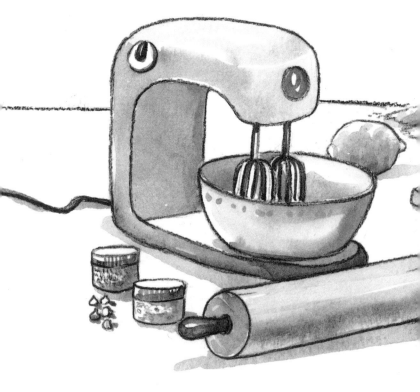

- $^3/_4$ cup butter (1$^1/_2$ sticks)
- 1 cup white sugar
- 2 eggs
- 1 teaspoon lemon extract
- 2$^1/_2$ cups all-purpose flour
- 1 teaspoon baking powder
- $^1/_2$ teaspoon salt

MAKE THE DOUGH:

1. Let the butter sit at room temperature until it is soft. This will take about an hour.
2. In a large bowl, mix the butter and sugar together until smooth.
3. Add the eggs and the lemon extract. Mix.
4. Stir in the flour, baking powder, and salt.
5. Cover the bowl with aluminum foil.
6. Chill the dough for at least one hour. (Longer is fine too. You can even leave it overnight.)

MAKE YOUR COOKIES:

1. Preheat the oven to 400 °F.
2. Lightly dust a smooth, clean surface with flour. (A kitchen counter works well.)
3. Roll out the dough until it's about ½ inch thick.
4. Cut into dog shapes with the cookie cutter.
5. Place the cookies 1 inch apart on the cookie sheets.
6. Decorate the cookies. (See ideas on the following pages.)
7. Bake the decorated cookies 6 to 8 minutes. Cool completely.
8. Eat!

HOW TO DECORATE YOUR COOKIES

• "Paint" your cookies with egg-yolk paint. Mix one egg yolk* with a teaspoon of milk or water. Divide into four small containers. Add red food coloring to the first cup. Stir well. Repeat to make blue, green, and yellow paint. Use a pastry brush or a clean, new paintbrush to paint the cookies. Try mixing the paints to make new colors. After baking, the paint will be shiny and brightly colored.

• Use raisins, red hots, or mini–chocolate chips to give your Fang cookies eyes, noses, and pretend fur.

• Sprinkle on chopped nuts or colored sugar.

*Nate is good at separating
eggs. Try it! Crack an egg over a bowl.
Open the shell slowly. Let the egg white fall into
the bowl while catching the yolk in half of the shell.
Gently pour the yolk into the empty half to separate
more egg white and let it fall into the bowl. You
should be left with just the yolk!

How to Make Lemonade

Fang cookies taste good with lemonade.
You can make your own.

Ask an adult to help you.

Makes one glass.

GET TOGETHER:

- one lemon
- a knife
- a glass
- ¼ cup of sugar
- a spoon
- ice cubes
- cold water

MAKE YOUR LEMONADE:

1. Cut the lemon in half.
2. Squeeze the lemon into the glass. Use a lemon squeezer if you have one. Or just use your hands.
3. Pour in the sugar. Stir well.
4. Add several ice cubes.
5. Fill the glass with cold water.
6. Enjoy!

Monster Jokes

What do you get when you cross the
Abominable Snowman and Dracula?
Frostbite!

What kind of dog does Dracula own?
A bloodhound!

Why doesn't Dracula have more friends?
Because he's a pain in the neck!

What is Dracula's favorite fruit?
Neck-tarines.

What is Dracula's favorite soup?
Scream of tomato.

What is Dracula's favorite animal?
The giraffe.

What did Frankenstein do with his lunch?
He bolted it down.

The Right Way to Recycle

Rosamond is not good at recycling.
You can be. Try these steps:

1. **LEARN** about the recycling program where you live. Most American cities have **curbside recycling.** That means you separate recyclables from the rest of your garbage and place them at the curb. Trash collectors pick them up. In some places, you may need to take your recyclables to a special center for collection.

2. **COLLECT** recyclable materials. These things are easy to recycle:
   - Newspapers, magazines, and other types of paper
   - Aluminum cans (like soda cans)
   - Steel cans (like soup cans)
   - Glass jars (like peanut butter or baby food jars)
   - Plastic bottles (like water or detergent bottles)

   Paper with food on it is NOT recyclable. Do not be like Rosamond. Throw your stinky fish paper away!

3. **TAKE THE STUFF OUT.** Carry your recyclables to the curb or visit the recycling center.

4. **FEEL GOOD ABOUT DOING YOUR PART!**

225

Have you helped solve all
Nate the Great's mysteries?

❑ **Nate the Great**: Meet Nate, the great detective, and join him as he uses incredible sleuthing skills to solve his first big case.

❑ **Nate the Great Goes Undercover**: Who— or what—is raiding Oliver's trash every night? Nate bravely hides out in his friend's garbage can to catch the smelly crook.

❑ **Nate the Great and the Lost List**: Nate loves pancakes, but who ever heard of cats eating them? Is a strange recipe at the heart of this mystery?

❑ **Nate the Great and the Phony Clue**: Against ferocious cats, hostile adversaries, and a sly phony clue, Nate struggles to prove that he's still the greatest detective.

❑ **Nate the Great and the Sticky Case**: Nate is stuck with his stickiest case yet as he hunts for his friend Claude's valuable stegosaurus stamp.

❑ **Nate the Great and the Missing Key**: Nate isn't afraid to look anywhere—even under the nose of his friend's ferocious dog, Fang—to solve the case of the missing key.

❑ **Nate the Great and the Snowy Trail**: Nate has his work cut out for him when his friend Rosamond loses the birthday present she was going to give him. How can he find the present when Rosamond won't even tell him what it is?

❑ **Nate the Great and the Fishy Prize**: The trophy for the Smartest Pet Contest has disappeared! Will Sludge, Nate's clue-sniffing dog, help solve the case and prove he's worthy of the prize?

❑ **Nate the Great Stalks Stupidweed**: When his friend Oliver loses his special plant, Nate searches high and low. Who knew a little weed could be so tricky?

❑ **Nate the Great and the Boring Beach Bag**: It's no relaxing day at the beach for Nate and his trusty dog, Sludge, as they search through sand and surf for signs of a missing beach bag.

❑ **Nate the Great Goes Down in the Dumps**: Nate discovers that the only way to clean up this case is to visit the town dump. Detective work can sure get dirty!

❑ **Nate the Great and the Halloween Hunt**: It's Halloween, but Nate isn't trick-or-treating for candy. Can any of the witches, pirates, and robots he meets help him find a missing cat?

❑ **Nate the Great and the Musical Note**: Nate is used to looking for clues, not listening for them! When he gets caught in the middle of a musical riddle, can he hear his way out?

❏ **Nate the Great and the Stolen Base**: It's not easy to track down a stolen base, and Nate's hunt leads him to some strange places before he finds himself at bat once more.

❏ **Nate the Great and the Pillowcase**: When a pillowcase goes missing, Nate must venture into the dead of night to search for clues. Everyone sleeps easier knowing Nate the Great is on the case!

❏ **Nate the Great and the Mushy Valentine**: Nate hates mushy stuff. But when someone leaves a big heart taped to Sludge's doghouse, Nate must help his favorite pooch discover his secret admirer.

❏ **Nate the Great and the Tardy Tortoise**: Where did the mysterious green tortoise in Nate's yard come from? Nate needs all his patience to follow this slow . . . slow . . . clue.

❏ **Nate the Great and the Crunchy Christmas**: It's Christmas, and Fang, Annie's scary dog, is not feeling jolly. Can Nate find Fang's crunchy Christmas mail before Fang crunches on *him*?

❏ **Nate the Great Saves the King of Sweden**: Can Nate solve his *first-ever* international case without leaving his own neighborhood?

❏ **Nate the Great and Me: The Case of the Fleeing Fang**: A surprise Happy Detective Day party is great fun for Nate until his friend's dog disappears! Help Nate track down the missing pooch, and learn all the tricks of the trade in a special fun section for aspiring detectives.

- **Nate the Great and the Monster Mess**: Nate loves his mother's deliciously spooky Monster Cookies, but the recipe has vanished! This is one case Nate and his growling stomach can't afford to lose.

- **Nate the Great, San Francisco Detective**: Nate visits his cousin Olivia Sharp in the big city, but it's no vacation. Can he find a lost joke book in time to save the world?

- **Nate the Great and the Big Sniff**: Nate depends on his dog, Sludge, to help him solve all his cases. But Nate is on his own this time, because Sludge has disappeared! Can Nate solve the case and recover his canine buddy?

- **Nate the Great on the Owl Express**: Nate boards a train to guard Hoot, his cousin Olivia Sharp's pet owl. Then Hoot vanishes! Can Nate find out *whooo* took the feathered creature?